Dear Parent:
Your child's love of reading starts here!

Every child learns to read in a different way and at his or her own speed. Some go back and forth between reading levels and read favorite books again and again. Others read through each level in order. You can help your young reader improve and become more confident by encouraging his or her own interests and abilities. From books your child reads with you to the first books he or she reads alone, there are I Can Read Books for every stage of reading:

SHARED READING
Basic language, word repetition, and whimsical illustrations, ideal for sharing with your emergent reader

BEGINNING READING
Short sentences, familiar words, and simple concepts for children eager to read on their own

READING WITH HELP
Engaging stories, longer sentences, and language play for developing readers

READING ALONE
Complex plots, challenging vocabular   ⅃ high-interest topics for the independent reader

ADVANCED READING
Short paragraphs, chapters, and for the perfect bridge to char

I Can Read Books have introdu   the joy of reading since 1957. Featuring award-winn.   illustrators and a fabulous cast of beloved characters, I ᴗ   Books set the standard for beginning readers.

A lifetime of discovery begins with the magical words **"I Can Read!"**

Visit www.icanread.com for information
on enriching your child's reading experience.

Pinkalicious®
and the Amazing Sled Run

To Kirsten!

—V.K.

The author gratefully acknowledges
the artistic and editorial contributions of
Daniel Griffo and Jacqueline Resnick.

I Can Read Book® is a trademark of HarperCollins Publishers.

Pinkalicious and the Amazing Sled Run
Copyright © 2018 by Victoria Kann

PINKALICIOUS and all related logos and characters are trademarks of Victoria Kann. Used with permission.

Based on the HarperCollins book *Pinkalicious* written by
Victoria Kann and Elizabeth Kann, illustrated by Victoria Kann
All rights reserved. Manufactured in the U.S.A.
No part of this book may be used or reproduced in any manner whatsoever without
written permission except in the case of brief quotations embodied in critical articles and reviews.
For information address HarperCollins Children's Books, a division of HarperCollins Publishers,
195 Broadway, New York, NY 10007.
www.icanread.com

Library of Congress Control Number: 2017962473
ISBN 978-0-06-267565-1 (trade bdg.)—ISBN 978-0-06-256696-6 (pbk.)

19 20 21 22 CWM 10 9 8 7 6 5 4 3
❖
First Edition

I Can Read!

BEGINNING READING **1**

Pinkalicious®
and the Amazing Sled Run

by Victoria Kann

HARPER
An Imprint of HarperCollinsPublishers

Snow was everywhere!

Pinkville looked like the North Pole.

"It's a snow day!" I cheered.

"Let's go sledding!" Peter said.

"I wish you could," said Mommy.

The snow was higher than the door!

"We're snowed in," I said.

"No we're not," said Peter.

He ran upstairs, and I ran after him.

"There's a sledding hill right here!"
I gasped.

"You're smart-errific!" I told Peter.

Peter and I grabbed our coats.

I climbed out the window

and onto the drift.

I was way up high!

"What a hill!" Peter said.

"I'll try it out," I said.

"Here I go!" I cheered.

The ride was over before I knew it.

"That was too short," I said.

"Then let's make the hill

longer," Peter said.

"We'll build a real sled run!"

We went inside to get shovels.

"Our sled run will be the

steepest in town," I told Peter.

"And the fastest!" he said.

We dug and carved the track.

Molly waved from next door.

"That looks like fun!" she said.

"I want to help!"

Everyone came out to help.

Finally, it was time to test

out our sled run!

Peter and I climbed back inside.

From our window,

I could see the whole hill.

"Pinkawow!" I said.

With so many friends helping,

our sled run had gotten very long.

It went through the whole town!

"Can I go first?" Peter begged.

He carried the sled to the window.

"The sled is going to fly

like a bird!" he said.

"It's going to speed

like a race car!

It's going to—"

He looked down and froze.

He made a strange little squeak.

"What's wrong?" I asked.

"I—I don't feel well," Peter said.

"Go without me," he said.

Peter's voice trembled.

I knew that voice.

It wasn't his sick voice.

It was his scared voice!

I knew just what I had to do.

"What do snowmen eat for lunch?"

I asked Peter.

"Icebergers!" I said.

Peter laughed.

"Do you feel better?" I asked.

"Much," Peter said.

"Then let's go sledding!" I said.

Peter's face went pale.

"I can't!" he said.

"The hill's so big," he said.

"It's too scary!"

"What if we go on the sled

together?" I asked.

"We can both fit!"

"I don't know," Peter said.

"You can hold on to me."

"It will be less scary together,"

I promised.

Peter took a deep breath.

"Okay," he agreed.

"Climb aboard the Pinkmobile!"

I said.

Peter held on tight.

"On your mark . . .

get set . . .

sled!" I said.

Whoosh!

Our sled went faster and faster.

We zipped left.

We zoomed right.

We flew past Alison's house
and Mr. Swizzle's ice-cream shop.

"No time to stop

for an ice-cream cone!" I said.

I could see the whole town.

"WHEEEEE!" I screamed.

Peter didn't say anything.

He was still scared.

Then I had an idea.

"Where does a polar bear

keep his money?" I asked Peter.

"In a snow bank!"

Peter laughed so hard

that he looked up.

We sped around a corner.

"Is this so bad?" I asked.

Peter didn't answer.

"WHEEEEE!" he said instead.

We slid to a stop in the park.

"What did you think?" I asked.

Peter gave me a big hug.

"Let's do it again!" he said.